Gekko Saves the City

Based on the episode
"Lionel-saurus"

Ready-to-Read

Simon Spotlight
New York   London   Toronto   Sydney   New Delhi

SIMON SPOTLIGHT
An imprint of Simon & Schuster Children's Publishing Division
1230 Avenue of the Americas, New York, New York 10020
This Simon Spotlight edition August 2018
Adapted by May Nakamura from the series PJ Masks
For information about special discounts for bulk purchases, please contact
Simon & Schuster Special Sales at 1-866-506-1949 or business@simonandschuster.com.
Manufactured in the United States of America 0718 LAK
10 9 8 7 6 5 4 3 2 1
ISBN 978-1-5344-1773-1 (hc)
ISBN 978-1-5344-1772-4 (pbk)
ISBN 978-1-5344-1774-8 (eBook)

Greg loves playing with
his pet lizard, Lionel.

Oh no!

Lionel is gone!

The PJ Masks need to find him!

Amaya becomes Owlette!

Greg becomes Gekko!

Connor becomes Catboy!

They are the PJ Masks!

The PJ Masks hear

a loud noise.

They run toward the sound.

Now the sound is coming
from behind them.

Who is there?

It is Lionel!

He is as big as a house!

Romeo gives strange treats
to Lionel.

Lionel grows even bigger!

"Lionel is out of control,"
says Catboy.

"He needs a leash,"
says Owlette.

Gekko thinks a leash is
a bad idea.

Lionel does not like
the leash.

He shakes it off.

Romeo wants Lionel to destroy Headquarters. "Climb!" Romeo says to Lionel.

Oh no!

Headquarters will fall down!

Gekko feels bad.

He should not have

put a leash on Lionel.

Lionel and Gekko are
friends.

Gekko has an idea.

He grabs a tree branch
with his Super Lizard Grip.

"Fetch, Lionel!"

Gekko says.

Lionel loves playing fetch!

He leaps off Headquarters.

"No!" Romeo wails.

His plan is ruined.

Lionel shrinks back
to his normal size.

"I love you, Lionel!"

Gekko says.

The PJ Masks save the day
and Lionel, too!